P9-CCS-521

HERGÉ

THE ADVENTURES OF TINTIN

Tintin in Tibet

LITTLE, BROWN AND COMPANY
BOSTON/NEW YORK/TORONTO/LONDON

Translated by Leslie Lonsdale-Cooper
and Michael Turner

The TINTIN books are published in the following languages :

Afrikaans :		HUMAN & ROUSSEAU, Cape Town.
Arabic :		DAR AL-MAAREF, Cairo.
Basque :		MENSAJERO, Bilbao.
Brazilian :		DISTRIBUIDORA RECORD, Rio de Janeiro.
Breton :		CASTERMAN, Paris.
Catalan :		JUVENTUD, Barcelona.
Chinese :		EPOCH, Taipei.
Danish :		CARLSEN IF, Copenhagen.
Dutch :		CASTERMAN, Dronten.
English :	U.K. :	METHUEN CHILDREN'S BOOKS, London.
	Australia :	REED PUBLISHING, Melbourne.
	Canada :	REED PUBLISHING, Toronto.
	New Zealand :	REED PUBLISHING, Auckland.
	Republic of South Africa :	STRUIK BOOK DISTRIBUTORS, Johannesburg.
	Singapore :	OCTOPUS ASIA, Singapore.
	Spain :	EDICIONES DEL PRADO, Madrid.
	Portugal :	EDICIONES DEL PRADO, Madrid.
	U.S.A.	LITTLE BROWN, Boston.
Esperanto :		CASTERMAN, Paris.
Finnish :		OTAVA, Helsinki.
French :		CASTERMAN, Paris-Tournai.
	Spain :	EDICIONES DEL PRADO, Madrid.
	Portugal :	EDICIONES DEL PRADO, Madrid.
Galician :		JUVENTUD, Barcelona.
German :		CARLSEN, Reinbek-Hamburg.
Greek :		ANGLO-HELLENIC, Athens.
Icelandic :		FJÖLVI, Reykjavik.
Indonesian :		INDIRA, Jakarta.
Iranian :		MODERN PRINTING HOUSE, Teheran.
Italian :		GANDUS, Genoa.
Japanese :		FUKUINKAN SHOTEN, Tokyo.
Korean :		UNIVERSAL PUBLICATIONS, Seoul.
Malay :		SHARIKAT UNITED, Pulau Pinang.
Norwegian :		SEMIC, Oslo.
Picard :		CASTERMAN, Paris.
Portuguese :		CENTRO DO LIVRO BRASILEIRO, Lisboa.
Provençal :		CASTERMAN, Paris.
Spanish :		JUVENTUD, Barcelona.
	Argentina :	JUVENTUD ARGENTINA, Buenos Aires.
	Mexico :	MARIN, Mexico.
	Peru :	DISTR. DE LIBROS DEL PACIFICO, Lima.
Serbo-Croatian :		DECJE NOVINE, Gornji Milanovac.
Swedish :		CARLSEN IF, Stockholm.
Welsh :		GWASG Y DREF WEN, Cardiff.

Artwork © 1960 by Casterman, Paris and Tournai
Library of Congress Catalogue Card Number Afo 33496
Translation Text © 1962 by Methuen & Co., Ltd., London
American Edition © 1975 by Little, Brown and Company (Inc.), Boston

All rights reserved. No part of this book may be reproduced in any form or by any electronic or mechanical means including information storage and retrieval systems without permission in writing from the publisher, except by a reviewer who may quote brief passages in a review.
Library of Congress catalog card no. 74-21621

20 19 18 17 16 15 14 13

Published pursuant to agreement with Casterman, Paris
Not for sale in the British Commonwealth

Printed by Casterman, S.A., Tournai, Belgium.

Tintin in Tibet

NEPAL AIR DISASTER
KATMANDU, Wednesday.—The D.C.3 missing since Monday on a flight from Patna to Katmandu is reported to have crashed in the Gosain Than massif.
It is believed that the aircraft, belonging to Indian Airways, was driven towards the Himalaya by a violent storm.
A search-plane yesterday spotted the wreckage of the aircraft in a remote and dangerous area. As soon as the news was received, a party of Sherpas set out for the peak where the aircraft crashed.
The aircraft is known to have carried 14 passengers and 4 crew.
BANDITS IN VIENNA RAID
Poor devils! What a dreadful place for a crash. They wouldn't stand a chance of surviving up there...
And that's what your beautiful mountains do for you!
DONG
The gong for dinner. Come on. I'm famished.
And after dinner...
Hmm! My queen's in danger. What shall I do? Protect her with my knight? No, that'd leave my bishop vulnerable. Suppose I advance that pawn?...
No, that won't work either... I shall have to do something else. Yes, my queen will have to fight a rearguard action... Right... then, with my next move I'll launch a flank attack with my other bishop... Then what will the enemy do? If he sees the danger, he'll cover his castle with a pawn...
In that case, I'll take the plunge and sacrifice my bishop. But he won't be sacrificed in vain! An eye for an eye: I shall take his castle... And there we are — check! Very neat! What do you say to that, eh Tintin?
CHANG!

Billions of blue blistering barnacles! You don't really have to sneeze like that, do you?
But... I... I... didn't sneeze.
I'm terribly sorry, I must have dropped off... I had a horrible nightmare...
A nightmare?
Yes. I was dreaming about Chang... you remember Chang, the boy I made friends with in China... I saw him... it was ghastly...
He was lying there hurt, half buried by snow... He was holding out his hands and calling to me, "Help, Tintin! help!" It was all so terribly real... I'm still quite stunned by it... Please do forgive me.
That's all right, don't worry. Forget it. You go on up to bed. You're dead tired.
I think you're right. Good night, Captain.
The next morning...
Hello there! Slept well?... No more dreams?
Good morning, Captain. No, no more dreams.
No dreams, but not much sleep, either. I was haunted by that picture of Chang lying in the snow, calling to me for help.
Rubbish! Dreams go by opposites, so they say. Don't think about it. Look, there's a letter for you, from Hong Kong.
Hong Kong?
Yes, look at the envelope. It's taken a long time to reach you. From Labrador Road to Marlinspike, then Nestor sent it on here.
Who's writing to me from Hong Kong?
BY AIR MAIL
PAR AVION
HONGKONG
丁丁先生台啟
比國布魯塞爾
香港張仲文
Please forward:
c/o Captain Haddock
Marlinspike Hall
Marlinspike
Mr. Tintin
Hotel des Sommets,
26, Labrador Road,
Vargèse
CHANG!

Honestly! Billions of blue blistering barnacles! You can't pretend this time that you've had another dream!
No, no! Look here: it really is a letter from Chang!
You must admit it's a remarkable coincidence. Yesterday evening I dreamt about him: this morning I get a letter from him. Extraordinary, isn't it?
Yes... I suppose so. What does he want, anyway?
Here, listen: "The brother of my most venerable adoptive father"... I didn't know that Mr. Wang Chen-Yee had a brother... "The brother of my most venerable adoptive father is living in London, where he has an antique shop. He has generously invited me to stay with him..." Hooray!
"Although unworthy of such an invitation I have accepted. Tomorrow I leave Hong Kong by air. I am filled with pleasure that I shall see your noble face once again". He's coming! Good!
Yes, fine... But, I say... this Chang, he's not like that little monster Abdullah, is he?
Chang? Why, Captain, he's one of the nicest people I know: quiet, unassuming - and with a heart of gold. You'll see!
Yes, and Chang's an old friend of yours too, isn't he, Snowy?
Professor Calculus! Wonderful news! Chang's coming! We're going to see CHANG again!
Champagne? At this hour!?
Chang's coming!... Tralala!
It is most reprehensible, Captain, to give this young man champagne, and in the morning too!
?
When's he coming, then... your... er... Son of Heaven?
Let's see.
He says: "I fly to Calcutta, then on to Nepal. My venerable adoptive father wishes me to visit Katmandu to pay my respects to his honourable cousin who has many children, and to take them presents."
Nepal?... Katmandu?... The plane that hit a mountain ... surely that was going to Katmandu?
Quick... this morning's paper. Perhaps there'll be some details of the crash.
Daily Reporter

There! "Nepal Air Disaster - No survivors."
addition to 4 members of the crew.
TRAGIC DELAY
Among the missing is a young Chinese, travelling from Hong Kong to London. He arrived in Patna in time for an earlier aircraft but failed to obtain a seat. Forced to wait overnight, he caught the ill-fated D.C.3. The victim of this tragic delay is Chang Chong-Chen, adopted son of Mr. Wang Chen-
Chang! ... My poor friend, Chang!
That's what comes of drinking too much champagne!
You...you and your champagne!
Chang! My dear friend Chang! We shall never see him again ... never again!
No, it isn't true!... I know... CHANG IS NOT DEAD!
Not dead ??
He's alive; I'm sure of it!... The accident happened days ago, but yesterday I saw Chang alive...calling for help, but alive!
But that was just a dream you had ... it wasn't real.
I know. But it wasn't an ordinary dream. It was... it was a sort of premonition ... telepathy... something like that. But one thing's certain; I know that Chang is alive.
Steady on, Tintin.
He's alive, I tell you! I'm packing my bag and leaving for Nepal.
What?... You?... Leaving for Nepal?
But look here, old fellow, it's madness!...
That's right! You go and sober up!
Tintin, listen. I can understand how grieved you are, and I realise how much that dream has shaken you, but you must be sensible...
I must save Chang!
Ten thousand thundering typhoons! How can you possibly save someone who's already dead?
Chang is not dead.
CHANG!
!
?

Chang, come here! How often must I tell you not to speak to common mongrels?
Blistering barnacles! What a daft idea, giving a name like that to a dog!
Not really: it's a pekingese, it's quite reasonable.
Look here, Tintin... If your friend Chang was still alive, then the rescue party would have found him.
Possibly...
A common mongrel! Me!!
Possibly!... Possibly!... All right, let's suppose that he is still alive. I...
!
?
CHANG
Do you really have to sneeze like that?
Excuse be, sir, but I'b got a terrible cold id by dose...
CHANG
As I was saying: even if he were alive, why should you be able to find him, when Sherpas and experienced mountaineers have failed?
Captain, I am convinced that Chang is alive. Maybe it's stupid, but there it is. And since I believe that he's alive, I'm going to look for him.
All right, be obstinate! Go to Nepal, go to Timbuctoo, go to Vladivostok for all I care! But you'll be on your own, remember; I'm not coming, and that's flat! And when I say no, I mean no!
Two days later, at New Delhi...
VT-DAO

A few minutes later...
The plane for Katmandu? ... Oh yes, calling at Patna. It leaves at 2·35 this afternoon, but from the other airport, Willingdon. The bus will take you there, unless you...
... would rather visit the city. You have three hours. You should be at the airport at 2.0 p.m. You will find your baggage there.
Thank you. We'll take your advice and have a look round the city.
A little later...
There's the Qutab Minar. It's 238 feet high.
...and the Red Fort.
Three hours have passed...
We still haven't seen the Jama Masjid and the Rajghat, the memorial to Mahatma Gandhi...
Yes, but aren't you forgetting the time?
INDIA GUIDE to DELHI
We've just got time to hop into a taxi and make a dash for the airport.
Pity!
Hello, there's a crowd down there. What's going on? A fight? Or an accident?...
A cow! She's certainly chosen a good spot... completely blocking the roadway.
I say, can't someone move the old girl along? We're in rather a hurry...
Sacred cow, Sahib... Do not disturb... You wait till she move.
Wait? That's a useful suggestion! Our plane leaves in twenty-five minutes.
Anyway, no need to worry: if she won't move we'll just step over her...
Hey! Whoa! Stop fooling around!
Hey!... Hi!... WHOA!... STOP!

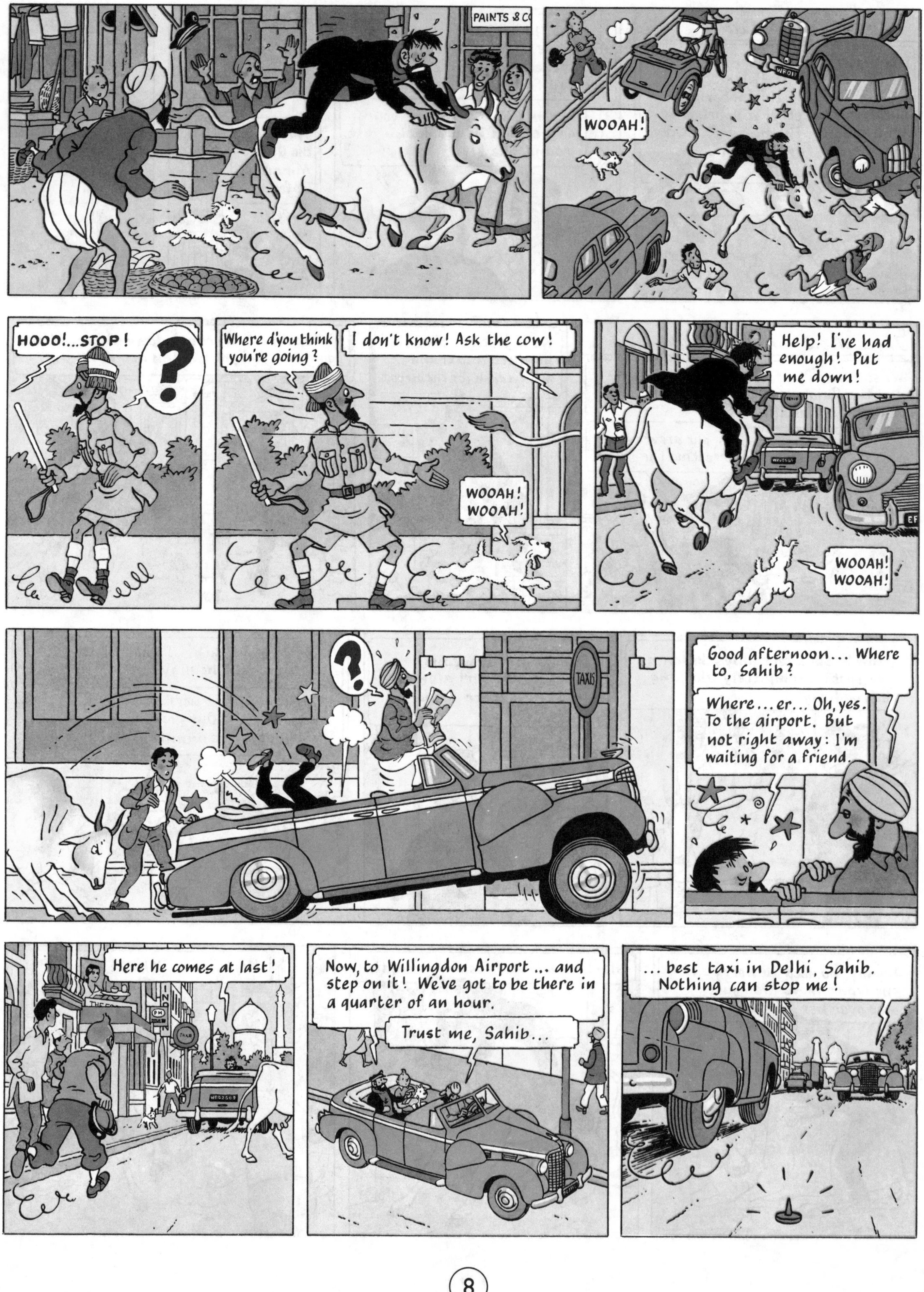
PAINTS & CO
WOOAH!
HOOO!...STOP!
?
Where d'you think you're going?
I don't know! Ask the cow!
WOOAH! WOOAH!
Help! I've had enough! Put me down!
WOOAH! WOOAH!
TAXIS
?
Good afternoon... Where to, Sahib?
Where... er... Oh, yes. To the airport. But not right away: I'm waiting for a friend.
Here he comes at last!
Now, to Willingdon Airport ... and step on it! We've got to be there in a quarter of an hour.
Trust me, Sahib...
... best taxi in Delhi, Sahib. Nothing can stop me!

Billions of blistering barnacles!
What's the matter?
Thundering typhoons! Something in my eye. I don't know what it is... dust, or a fly, or something. Stop, driver, stop!
No, I can't see anything. You'll have to wait until we're aboard the plane.
Carry on driver! And try to make up for lost time!
Right, Sahib.
Hey, my cap!
We go on like this, Sahib, and we never arrive in time.
At the airport...
Can't be helped: it's time for take-off. Too bad for the two missing passengers.
No, look: here they come.
Blue blistering barnacles! Confound this thing in my eye!
AIR INDIA
That's lucky: I can just see enough to get up the gangway...
AIR INDIA
Captain, stop! Not there! Here! The other steps!
And when I've finished, I'll see what's in your eye.
FIRST AID

The next morning...
This is Katmandu.
First of all we'll see the airport manager.
VT-D
There it is. We are friends of Chang, one of the victims of the Gosain Thar disaster. We want to visit the scene of the crash. You know all about the organisation of the search party: can you help us to achieve our object?...
Would it be indiscreet to ask the reason why you wish to go up there?
Because I am certain that Chang is not dead. I want to go and look for him.
But you must be mad. You have no conception of the difficulty and the danger such an expedition involves.
That rubber band's getting on my nerves.
Not only would you be risking your lives, but the risk would be quite futile. Even if your friend survived the accident he would long since have died from hunger and cold and exposure.
That's what I keep on telling him.
Ha! ha! ha! ha!
Oh, sorry!
Look, sir... Chang is my friend. In spite of all appearances, I know that he is still alive. Whatever the obstacles lying in our path, I must try to find him.
Very well... I'm quite certain no guide will agree to go with you. But if you wish, I'll put you in touch with the Sherpas who made up the rescue party.
I really am very grateful.
You see? Anybody with any sense thinks as I do: this idea of yours is absolutely crazy!
Chang is alive, Captain!
Chang is alive! Chang is alive! All this just because you had a dream about him! ... I dreamt about Columbus last night, but that doesn't bring him to life, does it? I don't behave like a sleep-walker, roaming around in a daze with my eyes shut!
Look out!
?

?!
Wake up, you milk-maid, and look where you're going!
LOOK OUT!
Billions of blistering barnacles in a thundering typhoon! You did that on purpose, you gang of Bashi-bazouks!
क्यों जी? देखते नहीं सामने क्या है?...
What's the matter, Captain? Met your match at last?
Come on. We'll ask these men... perhaps they know the shop kept by Chang's relation.
Excuse me, but can you direct me to a shop owned by a Chinese gentleman ... er...a Chinese shop?
Chinese shop?
I wonder what they are, those red mats over there.
Hello! It's fruit, spread out to dry in the sun. Mm! It smells good!
Fruit?... Good to eat?... Nice and sweet?... Yum-yum?
Yes, Sahib.
Yes, Sahib.
Chinese shop?... Up there, Sahib. You turn left. Then big temple... Then street right. There Chinese shop... Cheng Li is name.
Thank you very much.
FIRE!...

W-w-what happened? I ate one of those things. It was just like swallowing a volcano in full blast!
It was a red pimento, Captain... pepper! ...
A few minutes later...
There's the big temple he mentioned...
Wonderful, isn't it?
Good-day Sahib. My name Cheng Li-Kin. I think you are looking for me... Yes please.
Yes... but how did you know?
Yes please, Sahib. You ask someone the way, and he come and tell me... Yes? ...
Please to do me the inexpressible honour of taking a humble cup of tea in my miserable house. Yes please?
We'd be glad to. Yes please.
Mr. Cheng, we are friends of Chang ...
Friends of Chang?... So?... Yes please!... He will have great happiness to see you.

What... what did you say?
Great happiness to see you. Please to enter: we are here...
CHANG! CHANG! Some friends for you.
My son, Chang Lin-Yee... Yes please.
We're so sorry: there has been a mistake. Our friend is called Chang Chon-Chen.
Ah, you speak of our late lamented adoptive nephew... Yes please.
Alas! he is dead... Yes please... in aeroplane crash.
So we have heard. But I believe that Chang is not dead. I have come to ask ... Do you know of a Sherpa who'd agree to go with us to search for Chang?
Even though he is dead?
I do not believe that. But I need an experienced guide if I am to find him.
Why not Tharkey, respected father? He is the best Sherpa in the district, and the bravest. Also, he went with the rescue party.
We go to him, if you wish. But I tell you his answer.
NO, SAHIB!
No! Me not want to risk three lives - your life, life of the other Sahib, and my life - to look for dead man.
But you see, Tharkey, I am convinced that Chang isn't dead.
Him dead, Sahib!... I go there. I see broken aeroplane. No one alive. Not possible to live: too cold, nothing to eat. You not go, Sahib, you too young to die as well.
It's only common sense, old lad. The Sherpa is absolutely right. I've told you from the very begining, it's sheer lunacy. You really must give up this daft idea.
Yes, what Tharkey says is true.
Fine! You're talking sense at last!

It's true: I have no right to risk the lives of others.
Bravo! I knew you'd see reason.
I shall go alone.
!?
All right! ... Go! ... But on your own! I've trailed along this far, thundering typhoons, but I'm not playing nurse-maid any longer!
Look out, Captain!
Billions of bilious blue blistering barnacles! Has the word gone around to gang up on me? ...
?!?
क्या? फिर वही?
Please, please... Watch your language! I didn't shout at you did I?
Three days later...
There. That's my rucksack packed. Now I'll just say goodbye to the Captain.
I don't like the look of all these preparations.
RAT TAT TAT
YES?
!
?
I... I've come to say goodbye. But... your rucksack... What ...?
D'you imagine for one moment that I'd let a young whippersnapper like you go off alone? Not on your life! I suppose you think that Captain Haddock has got tomato juice in his veins, eh? ...
But you...
But, but, but... don't start being awkward! I'm going with you, whether you like it or not. And not another word from you, or I stay here!
Now who is it? Come in!
RAT TAT TAT
!?

Hey, you're the rogue who knocks me down at every street corner. Blistering barnacles, what do you want now ?!
Sherpa Tharkey send me, Sahib.
He say : everything ready. I am porter, Sahib.
Then we shall have fun! ... Good, tell Tharkey we are coming.
You're wondering what's going on ? Well, you insisted on going, so I had another crack at Tharkey. I was luckier than you were the other day: I persuaded him to take us up there.
Captain, what can I say ? You're a marvel!
Not so fast, not so fast! He's only agreed to take us as far as the wreck of the aircraft: no further. Still, once you're up there, at last you'll realise there isn't the remotest chance of finding any-one alive.
All the same, Tharkey has fixed up everything we need for the expedition: clothes, food, equip-ment and porters... But thun-dering typhoons, just my luck to be saddled with that fellow who behaves like a bull in a china shop!
An hour later...
Just think, here am I, fooling around at the back end of Nepal when I could be snooz-ing at Marlinspike, with a long, cool whisky at my elbow.
Whisky, by thunder! What about those bottles in my pack?
The grand old Duke of York ♩ ♫ He had ten thousand men... ♪ pom pom ♪ ♩

Great snakes!... He's off at full throttle!... Captain!... Hey, Captain, not so fast!
We let him go... Road is long... Soon catch him up... You not worry!
... and he marched ♫ ♪ them down, hic, again ♫ ♪
Z Z Z... Z Z Z... Z Z Z
Hello, Professor, what are you doing here?
Lost my umbrella.
Your umbrella? Why, I've got a ship-load of them here... Heaven knows where they've come from.
Rubbish! This is a red pimento!
Check mate!
I... I don't know... I must have fallen asleep on my feet... The heat, I expect... I think I was dreaming...
That night...
Thundering typhoons, my poor feet. I expect they'll be better in the morning... Goodnight, everybody.
Goodnight, Sahib.
Goodnight, Captain.
Ah, my beauty ♫ past compare: these jewels bright ♪ I wear!... ♪
?
!
!

Bianca Castafiore!... She's HERE, by thunder! That woman follows us to the ends of the earth!
Radio in porters' tent, Sahib.
Was I ever ♫ Margarita? ♩ Is it I?
He's right, by thunder! Well, I'll give them something to listen to!
Mind the guy-ropes, Captain.
Thanks!
Come reply! Come reply! Tell me, ♫ Tell me truly!
Now then, you musical morons - just you pack up that confounded juke-box... and jump to it! Understand?
Thundering typhoons, can't a man get a moment's peace... anywhere?
ZZOINNG
?
Billions of blistering barnacles! It's about time they made a tent to stay up without all these fiddling bits of string!!
Next morning...
... with Haddock leading the rest of the field!
Oho! The river... across we go!
With my usual good fortune, this should end with a loud splash!
But this time I shan't give them the pleasure...
There! Just a few more yards, and I've made it!
Good heavens! The Captain!
SPLASH

Chucking stones in the river! ... What a fright he gave us!
SPLASH
Yoohoo!
Look at me! Over already, without getting my feet wet either! How's that?
A remarkable performance, Captain! Congratulations! Just one thing: this isn't where we cross the river. Tharkey said the second bridge!
WHAT?
Billions of blistering barnacles!
Will he? Won't he?
Great snakes!
He will...
No... pity!
Well done, Captain. That's the safest way.
Not worth watching now ...
Just a bark or two, and you can change my name to Snowy!
Later ...
Golly, I could do with a drink.
That's lucky! A puddle of water.
Funny, that water tasted odd!
Wretched animal! What did you drink?
?

You unhappy creature! It was whisky!... Alcohol! Dragging an animal down to the level of man!
So what? Feels good, doesn't it? ...Warms the cockles of your heart, eh?
What about some more?... Look- all that whisky, dripping away...
Ho!... Dog! Dog!... Look!... Look at dog!
?
Dog, him drunk! Ha! ha! ha!
!
?
Poor Snowy. He must be feeling the height.
Look out!
Look out!
What are those four all shouting about?...Something wrong?
SNOWY!

Great snakes! He'll be dashed to pieces on the rocks!
No, he's fallen in the water! What luck!
SPLASH
There, he's come up again!
To the bridge! It's our one chance of saving him!
If only I'm in time...
There! Now I've got him!
A little later...
Oh, there you are. So you managed to rescue the old drunkard?
Drunkard?
Yes! And you thought he had mountain sickness! Look: a broken whisky bottle in my rucksack... But it didn't all run to waste!
!
And what's more, if this ever happens again I shan't risk my neck sav- ing you!
The long march goes on...
That is chorten, Sahib. Ashes of great lamas preserved there.
Stop, Sahib! Is bad luck!
Stop!
?
Ho!
?
Stop!

Well, what's up? Something the matter? What have I done?
It brings you bad luck, Sahib, if you pass right of a chorten.
Why? Am I breaking the Highway Code? Is this a one-way street?
Spirits are angry if man pass to right of chorten, Sahib. Then porters not dare to go on.
All right, all right, if it makes you happy.
Left or right, it's all the same to me, you know...
Look out, Captain!
Stop, Captain! Stop! Stop!
Nothing I'd like better!
Keep to the left, Sahib!
Keep to the left! Keep to the left! I'd like to see you do it!
My whisky ... safe ... That's the main thing!
ZZING

The next morning...
You'd think we were in an Alpine forest.
Two hours later...
I wouldn't mind rhododendrons like these at Marlin-spike!
And that afternoon...
?
SPLOTCH
It's some sort of rotten fruit: it dropped from a tree.
I wonder which one it came from?
SPLOTCH
The following night...
We camp here, Sahib.
Look, we've reached the snow.
Across there, Tibet! Aeroplane wreck there. Tomorrow we arrive. Now, we eat. Tsampa is ready.
Tsampa? What's this stuff made of?
Tsampa, Sahib: cooked barley meal, with tea and butter.
HAW-HAWAAAW
What's that noise?
Yeti!
That... that... that is yeti!!
The yeti! The Abominable Snowman!!
WO-OW

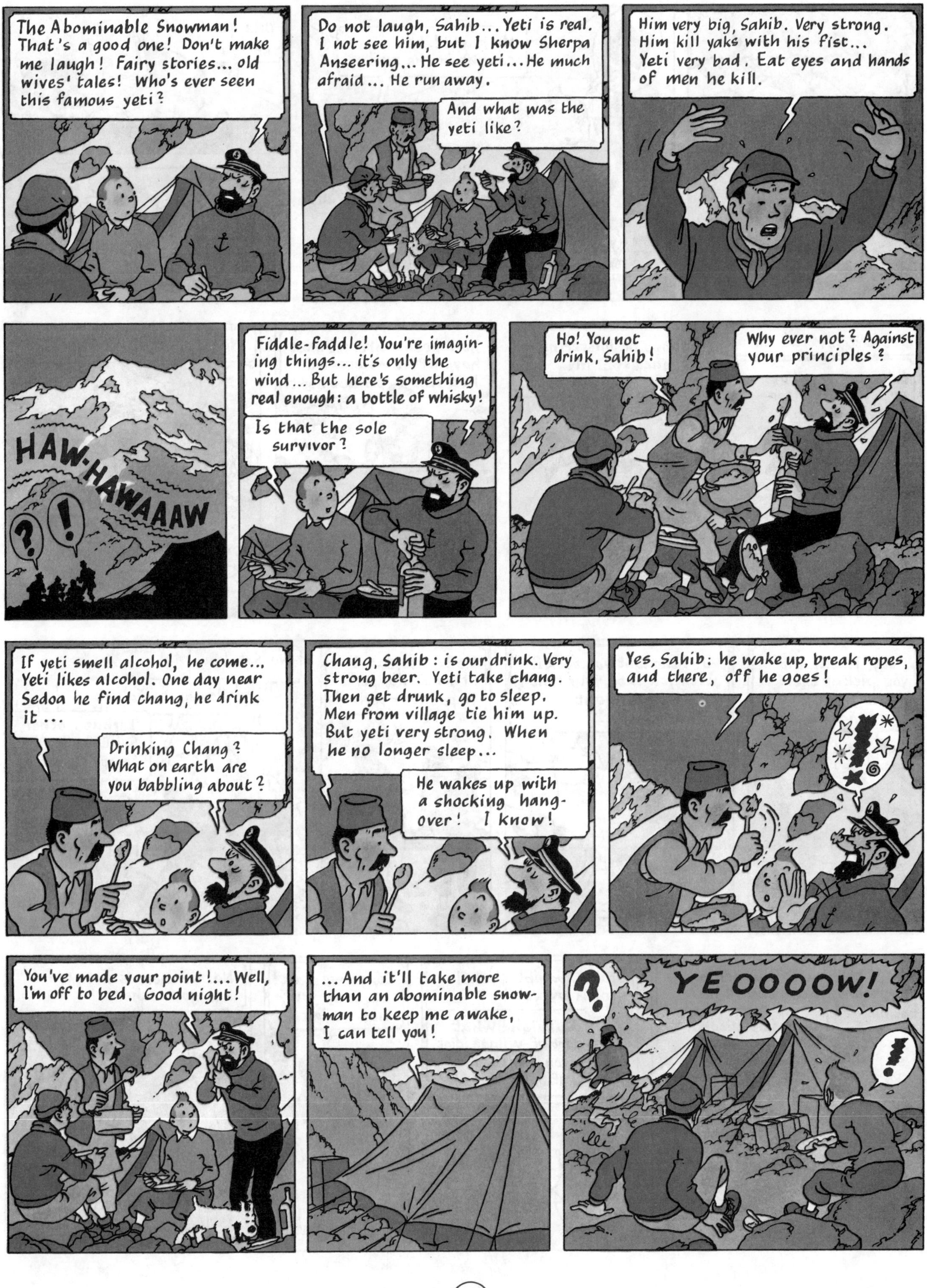

The Abominable Snowman! That's a good one! Don't make me laugh! Fairy stories... old wives' tales! Who's ever seen this famous yeti?
Do not laugh, Sahib... Yeti is real. I not see him, but I know Sherpa Anseering... He see yeti... He much afraid... He run away.
And what was the yeti like?
Him very big, Sahib. Very strong. Him kill yaks with his fist... Yeti very bad. Eat eyes and hands of men he kill.
HAW-HAWAAAW
?
!
Fiddle-faddle! You're imagining things... it's only the wind... But here's something real enough: a bottle of whisky!
Is that the sole survivor?
Ho! You not drink, Sahib!
Why ever not? Against your principles?
If yeti smell alcohol, he come... Yeti likes alcohol. One day near Sedoa he find chang, he drink it...
Drinking Chang? What on earth are you babbling about?
Chang, Sahib: is our drink. Very strong beer. Yeti take chang. Then get drunk, go to sleep. Men from village tie him up. But yeti very strong. When he no longer sleep...
He wakes up with a shocking hang-over! I know!
Yes, Sahib: he wake up, break ropes, and there, off he goes!
You've made your point!... Well, I'm off to bed. Good night!
...And it'll take more than an abominable snowman to keep me awake, I can tell you!
?
YEOOOOW!
!

YEEOOOW!
?!
My beard! It's caught in the zip!
CALCUTTA DG
One quick jerk, perhaps...
Got it!
EEK!
At daybreak...
I don't know, but... er... haven't I forgotten something?
Billions of blistering barnacles!... My bottle of whisky!
Now I remember; I must have left it where we had supper last night.
No!... But it WAS here...
GRRR
I say, Tintin. Did you pick up the bottle I left over there last night?
Me?
No. I thought you took it with you into your tent... What about Tharkey?...
Me?... No, Sahib. Other Sahib, perhaps?... Or porter?
No, Sahib.
No see it, Sahib.
Perhaps other Sahib? Or Sherpa Tharkey?
No, I tell you... Thundering typhoons, it can't have just vanished!
No, Sahib, alcohol not vanished...
Stolen, Sahib! Alcohol stolen by yeti!
Rubbish! what sort of village idiot d'you take me for? Half-baked Haddock?
Come, we start!... Long journey today.
No. No more start. We not go further.

Blistering barnacles, what's this? You won't go on?... What sort of pantomime is it this time?
We not go on, Sahib. We go home to our village.
We not want to be killed by yeti! ... Him drink Sahib's alcohol; make him very bad now!...
I know, I know, the yeti walked off with my whisky... D'you think I'm soft in the head?
Thundering typhoons, not only do these Bashi-bazouks refuse to go on, they expect me to swallow their hocus-pocus into the bargain!
I speak with them...
The yeti drinking whisky! I expect he plays the bagpipes too!
Well?... Any luck?... My whisky?
They not know... But they go on. I say, they have chicken-hearts: when they come home all the village laugh at them... And then I tell them, Sahib is very generous ... We go on.
Hey, Tintin!... What's up with that dog of yours? Look at him.
Snowy? Why?
Hey, Snowy! What's the matter?
GRRR
?
?
OH!
Look! Footmarks!... The Abominable Snowman!!
GRRR GRRRR

Tell me another! Have you fallen for that too?... Those footmarks were made by a bear. It's well known—bears do walk upright on their hind legs sometimes.
Anyway, we'll soon see... All we have to do is follow the tracks.
No, Sahib. You not do that! Be careful!
Be careful!... Be careful! ... This yeti nonsense is beginning to get on my nerves!
Billions of bilious blue blistering barnacles! My bottle of whisky!
EMPTY!
RKRPXZKRMTFRZ!
My whisky, you Cro-Magnon!... My whisky, you Mameluke, you!... Vampire!... Dipsomaniac!... Body-snatcher!
You odd-toed ungulate!... Macrocephalic baboon!... Phylloxera!... Cannibal!
Diplodocus!... Filibuster!... Megalomaniac!
Come on, you old alcoholic, unless you're too scared!
Do not shout, Sahib ... Avalanches!
Colocynth!... Troglodyte!... Pithecanthropus!

Kleptomaniac!...
Quick!... More snow may fall...
Ectoplasm!
OH!... Porters all gone!
!
!
YOOEE!
You come back, you poltroons!
poltroons...
troons...
...oons
I wasn't addressing you up there!
That's not the yeti; it's the echo!
No answer... They see the footmarks of yeti; very frightened; they return home to village. Now we cannot go on.
Abandoning ship! ...The lily-livered bandicoots!
?
But we simply must go on, Tharkey. We can't give up now, when we are so close to our goal.
Impossible, Sahib; we cannot carry porters' loads.
We'll each take an extra load; anything that isn't absolutely essential can be dumped here... Tharkey, we've got to save Chang!
...

Next morning...
Nearly there...
Look... Aeroplane crash... down below.
Now you see... no one living here, Sahib.
Here, no...
Is it not true, Sahib?... Not possible to find anyone here ... still alive.
It looks that way to me, and no mistake!
?
Look here!

It could have been Chang's... a present for his cousins...
Poor Chang! Why did you have to find that, of all things...
POOOOT
Careful, Sahib: avalanches!
Hello... Snowy seems to have found something to eat...
That's what he thinks!
Oh boy! This'll taste good!
GRRR
Poor old Snowy! You'll never manage it!... That chicken's frozen absolutely solid!
?
GRRR
GRRR
We camp here tonight, Sahib... Tomorrow return to the valley.
Well... I'm going to have a look around, over there, towards that rock-face...
... Because if I'd been in Chang's place, and I'd come out of the crash alive, that's where I would have headed...
I say, don't you think it's about time we had a breather?
... I'd have looked for a niche, or a cave, or a crack in the rock where I could shelter... But if that's what Chang did, why didn't he come out...
... when the rescue party arrived?... That's what puzzles me... Unless...
The mouth of a cave!
?
GRRR

Wait for a minute, while our eyes get accustomed to the dim light... Stop growling, Snowy.
GRRR
WIUUUUW
!
No, it's only the wind getting up...
There's something carved on this flat rock... What does it say?
CHANG! ... His name in Chinese! And he's carved it in our script too!...
TCHANG
So I wasn't mistaken! Chang did survive the accident... Chang sheltered here... But in heaven's name, what has become of him? Don't tell me he's here, quite close, in a dark corner of the cave!
CHANG!
CHANG!
BING BANG
!
WOOAH!
Great snakes! When I shouted it made some bits of ice fall.
BING
WOOAH!
It's no use. We must come back with torches. I'd better hurry and join the others.
Heavens! It's snowing!
This is awful! You can't see ten feet ahead...
Two hours later...
Still nothing, Sahib!

This is crazy! I ought to have waited in the cave till it stopped. I've completely lost my bearings now.
COOEE!
No good!... Not a sound! The noise of the wind is drowning my voice. And it's getting dark, too. What'll become of us now, Snowy?
Only one thing to do... go on.
!
A crevasse! Crumbs, Snowy, that was a near thing!
!
We must be careful now. Keep close behind me Snowy, old boy.
Saved!... Someone's there!... Yes, look, it's the Captain!
GRRR
AHOY! CAPTAIN!
CAPTAIN!... HI! CAPTAIN!
He can't hear me!... This is awful! ... CAPTAIN!
!
CAP.....
?
Two hours pass by...
WOWOOOWOOOWOOW

It seems to be easing up a bit.
Sh!... Listen, Sahib!
WOWOOWOOW
Yeti!
Is he still around?
WOWOOWOOW
I advise him to keep his distance, the drunken old ape!
But that's no yeti... It's something else; I've heard that cry before... Let's go outside; we'll hear it better there.
WOWOOWOOW...
Listen!
Snowy!... It's Snowy, howling for the dead! Something must have happened to Tintin!
Tharkey, we must go and search for him at once!
I fetch ropes and torches, Sahib. We go immediately.
WOWOOW... WOWOW
There!
Snowy!... My poor Snowy! Where's your master? What's happened to your master?
WOW...
Here, Sahib!... Fallen into crevasse!
Thundering typhoons!
TINTIN! TINTIN!

No answer! We simply must try to get him out of there, Tharkey!
You lower me into the crevasse, Sahib. I show you what to do.
Right.
You don't let go, eh, Sahib?
Don't you worry, Tharkey!
Captain!... Ahoy there, Captain!
Don't bother me now!... Can't you see I'm busy?...
But... who said that?
Tintin!... Hooray, it's Tintin!
The rope! Don't let go of the rope!
The rope, Captain!...
The rope? OH!!!
A little later...
I slid down. I bounced against the sides – luckily they were smooth. Then I hit my head against something hard, and I was knocked out.
When I came to, I crawled along the bottom of the crevasse – it gradually sloped upwards. Then, after a few acrobatics, I managed to get out... That was after I saw you, Captain, only a dozen yards away from me.
But there's one thing I just don't understand... How could you have passed so close to me in the blizzard, and yet not have seen me? You never even heard me, either, though heaven knows I shouted loud enough!
Me?... But I never budged from the plane.
Oh. Then it was you, Tharkey?
Me?... No, Sahib. Not me... I not move away from aeroplane.
But then... WHO was it that I saw?

You saw yeti, Sahib!... No doubt!... We go down quickly to valley. Great danger for us... Besides, no one alive up here...
But there is, Tharkey!
In an ice cave I discovered a stone on which Chang had carved his name... It absolutely proves that he survived the crash. I couldn't find anything more without a light. But as soon as we've taken care of Snowy, I suggest we all go and explore the cave.
Chang's name!... Then you were right after all!
At daybreak...
It was somewhere about here. But the snow last night has completely altered the landscape.
No, it wasn't as far as this... We must have passed the cave without noticing... Back again!
Look here, blistering barnacles, we've been going for two hours! Let's have a rest!
Later!
You can go on if you want to! I'm going to stop and sit down.
?
Here's your cave for you! When I start searching, I do the job properly!
Look: there's the stone I told you about.
But if Chang alive, Sahib, where is he now?
That's what I'm wondering, Tharkey.
I tell you, Sahib: your friend come here, yes... But afterwards, yeti kill him, and eat him up.
?
No Tharkey. In that case there'd be... it's too horrible... some traces of... of the tragedy.
!

Oh, Sahib! See!
!
No, thank heaven! It's the bone of an animal, like a chamois. But there should be others. Quick, let's look!
No, these are the bones of birds and small rodents.
Golly, this old yeti keeps a well-stocked larder!
But yeti perhaps eat Chang somewhere else... And how we find your friend under the snow?
I'm beginning to get a bit sick of this yeti business...
Ten thousand thundering typhoons, I wish he'd show up! Great flat-footed grizzly bear: I'd give him yeti!
We go back, Sahib. Nothing more to do here... Your friend dead, I am sure, Sahib.
Come on out, you big-head!
And Sahib, even if Chang alive...
...where can we search for him?... Where, Sahib? This way?
... Or that way?
I know, Tharkey. You're quite right: we must accept the evidence. Tomorrow we'll start making our way back to the valley.
The next morning ...
Come on Tintin, old lad. You've done everything humanly possible... Come on now ...
Goodbye, Chang! ... Goodbye!

Come along! No good hanging about.
!
Tharkey! ... Captain!... Stop!... Don't go! What's that yellow thing, up there, on the rock-face? ...
Something yellow? ... Where can you see something yellow?
Up there! Follow the direction of my finger ...
Quick! Give me my glasses. In the right-hand pocket of my rucksack.
A bit of rag ... No, a scarf!
Look there, Tharkey; a yellow scarf!... Caught on a rock ...
You're right, Sahib!
A scarf; where?
It's absolute proof that Chang is alive. He's even shown us the way up to find him. Come on, Tharkey, let's go!
Well, I can't see anything!
No, Sahib. I not go on. I promised to guide Sahibs to the aeroplane. I keep my word. Now I go down, for I am sure Chang is dead.
But the scarf, Tharkey?
No proof, Sahib... Only real climber could scale such a rock-face, Sahib.
Where the devil did those jokers see a scarf, anyway?
Need special boots, ropes, and other things. Chang not have those; he cannot climb up there.
What about the scarf?
But where is this precious scarf?
I not know how it comes up there ... in a storm, perhaps?... Or with yeti, perhaps? But not with Chang, Sahib ... Not Chang ... Chang dead, Sahib!
?
Thundering typhoons, there he is! ... It's him!

Blistering yetis, it's the barnacle! ... I mean... Yettering barnacles, it's the blister... up there... I mean... the yeti!
I can't see it ... Are you sure you...?
Sure I'm sure! ... A sort of enormous monkey... with a huge head like a coconut. He must have sensed that he'd been spotted; he bolted like a rabbit!
Well, yeti or no yeti, I'm going on. And you, Captain?
It's sheer lunacy, but I'll go with you. I've got a little score to settle with that pithecanthropic pickpocket up there!
And you, Tharkey ... you?
No, Sahib, I not follow you. Very brave, Sahib, but you not know mountain dangers. Very foolish, Sahib...
Perhaps... Well, Tharkey, in that case this is where we part... But first we must settle up... The Captain will do it ...
You do it, Tintin. I'm going to brew up.
Can you manage it, Captain?
Why not? It's as easy as pie. A child of three could do it. Perfectly simple...
Let's see... Five sevens are thirty-five; carry three. Five eights are forty: plus three, forty-three; carry four...
Don't forget the family allowances, and the national insur...
BOOM
WOW! OW!
A few minutes later...
Goodbye, Tharkey, and very many thanks. We couldn't have had a better guide.
Goodbye! ... I hope you one day return to your own country!
Thanks, Tharkey... Goodbye!
Now, on our way. ... First objective: the yellow scarf!
Hey, Captain, what are you doing?

What am I doing? ...Simple enough. I'm joining Tharkey. I'm going back with him.
But you agreed to go on...
Maybe, but now I've changed my mind... It's crazy to go ahead without a guide. I don't want to leave my bones in this benighted country!
Wait a minute.
Would you mind getting the flask in the back pocket of my rucksack? I'm terribly cold. A drop of brandy would set me right.
Did you say... er... brandy? You've still got some brandy?
Oh, it's only a little bottle I was keeping in reserve... Perhaps you'd like a drop too, Captain?
Would I? What a question!
GLUG
GLUG
Oh dear, it's empty already!
What about me?
Well, you know, alcohol is very bad for young people like you!... It's... it's deadly p-p-poison... Believe me, Tintin, there's n-n-nothing like t-t-total ab-ab-abstinence! Come along, now we-we-we'll rejoin Thar-Thar-Tharkey.
You know, Captain, on second thoughts, you're right to follow Tharkey. Better to give up... much wiser. The risk is far too great... In the first place, there's the yeti... It's just too bad if he thinks we've got cold feet...
WHAT?
C-c-cold f-feet?... Who has?... M-me?... S-s-scared of a ye-ye-yeti?... About turn, young fellow-me-lad... About t-t-turn!... Blistering barnacles, j-j-jump to it!
That did the trick!
Cold feet!... I'll sh-sh-show him, the scarecrow. I'll show him the sort of st-st-stuff Haddock's made of!
Not so fast!
C-c-cold feet!... ME!
Wait for me, Captain; we must rope up!
I suppose they think I've got wings!
Rope up yourself!... C-c-cold feet! Me!... Thundering ty-ty-typhoons! Let me tell you, when I-I-I meet your ye-ye-yeti the s-s-sparks will fly!
STOP!
E-E-E-EEK!
?

Tintin!... Tintin!... My ice-axe! What's happening?
It's nothing, Captain; just St. Elmo's fire. It's not dangerous. You're a sailor, surely you know it - an atmospheric phenomenon which sometimes makes flashes round the mast-head.
Thank goodness! I thought I'd turned into a sparking plug!
Wait for me this time; I'm coming.
First of all we're going to rope up. Then I'll jettison some of my load, so I can take Snowy up on my back.
Twenty minutes later ...
We made it!... Here's the scarf!
Oh, Captain! Look at it! Bloodstains!
Yes, I can see... But even supposing that this is Chang's scarf, what then? ... What do you suggest we do now, eh?
Go on, Captain... Chang came this way. We must follow this pathway to the top.
You call this a pathway!? ... Oh, all right.
Careful, Captain. This is rather tricky.
To think there are people who do this for fun!
!

YOW!!
Blistering barnacles! That was a near thing ... But I'm safe, thanks to you, .. and the rope. Amazing stuff, nylon! ... Now, can you haul me up towards you? ...
No such luck! If I make the slightest move, it's the high dive for us both!
Blistering barnacles! What are we going to do now?
And, thundering typhoons, there's no way of regaining a foothold on that perishing rock-face.
Poor Captain. He obviously doesn't realise - with each jerk the rope cuts further into me.
It's hopeless... I can't make it! And I'm beginning to freeze on the end of this bit of string ... Can you hang on up there?
For as long as possible... But I can feel myself getting weaker, and paralysed with cold.
Which means we both fall! That's no good, young fellow. You, at least, can save yourself. You must cut the rope: it's the only answer!
Never! Either we're both saved, or we die together! ...
You're talking nonsense! Better for one to die, rather than two, isn't it? ... Cut the rope, Tintin!
Never, you hear me? ... I'll never do that!
All right, I'll do it myself ... Get my knife ... and that's it ... Cast off moorings!
Thundering typhoons! ... I can't get the confounded blade open! My fingers are completely numb ... Ah, that's it! ...

Captain, I implore you! Don't do it! You're mad!
No! Blistering barnacles! My mind is made up!
Oh! Clumsy fool!
?!
YOOO-E-E
YOOO-E-E
?
YOOO-E-E
It's Tharkey's voice! ... Tharkey! ... We're saved!
A few moments later ...
But tell us, Tharkey; what were you doing - to find us here?
I go towards my village, but I think of you... You, young white sahib risking your life to save Chinese friend ... Me yellow man, like him, but I not want to help... I tell myself I am coward. I turn back, and follow you ...
Good for you, Tharkey!... Shall we go on together now?
That night...
Pitch camp quick behind rocks; storm comes!
Hold tight! I bring stones to fix tent!
Hurry, Tharkey!
HELP! The tent!...
Blistering barnacles! Let go!... Let go!

The tent's gone! ... Blown away!... Lost in the night!
Ssh!... You listen!
HAW-HAW-HAW
Yeti!!
What's that jackass doing out of doors at this hour?
HAW-HAW-HAW!...
HAW-HAW-HAW-HAW
THUMP
?
?
HOUI! HOUI! HOUI! HOUI! HOUI!
What's happened? He must have hurt himself.
Serves him right!
Houi... Houi... Houi...
We pitch my little tent for tonight. It is only tent for one. Very difficult for three to come in ...
We'll never all get inside this!
Well, we've got to!
Try to squeeze up a bit more, Captain!
A fat lot of use that is!... We're already packed like sar...aaar ... aaaaaar....
AAAAA ARTCH...
No, Captain, no! You musn't!...
TCHOOO

That is big, big disaster! If now we stay here, we freeze. We must move...
We go down now fast as possible ... We cannot spend more time seeking Chang.
Oh, Chang!
Two days later ...
This is it: I've had enough. For three days we've been on the go, without sleep. I'm done: I'm not moving another step.
Come on, Captain, just one last effort. In a few hours we'll be below the snow-line.
No. Go on without me.
I've still got a little brandy left. Here, come on, have a drop.
I don't care. Even if you fill me up with jet fuel, I won't budge another inch!
Tintin Sahib!... Tintin Sahib! ... Look!
A monastery!... We're saved!
There we can sleep, Sahib!
Get up, Captain! A monastery!
It'd take more than an earth-quake to shift me!
CRACK
Look out! We not stop here!
CRACK

BROOMMM
BROOMM
The White Goddess is angry! It is a portent.
Really, Blessed Lightning, you're as gullible as a Poh-Pryang peasant! It's an avalanche; neither more nor less.
!?
Look, Blessed Lightning ascends into the air. He is going to have another vision!
Blessed Lightning and his visions!... When you think, he's as blind as a bat from Wei-Pyiong!
Silence, Shining Light! Blessed Lightning speaks!
I see three men... no, two men and a young boy with a great heart... And a little dog, white as powder snow... They are in mortal danger...
Great Heart is walking... walking ... walking... He is at the end of his strength... Great Heart falls...
YEOW!...
WOWOOWOOW
MMMH...

What a terrible monster!... It's going to eat Tintin!
?
EEK!
Wooah! Wooah!
A yak! It nearly strangled me!
I must save the others! I must reach that monastery, at all costs ...
No, it's hopeless. With this twisted ankle I can't go on ... Oh, what can I do ? ... What can I do ?
Snowy! It's up to you to save us now, Snowy ... You must carry this message and get help from the monastery ...
Go, Snowy, go! ... Our lives depend upon you! Go on, quickly!
This message!... Carry this message... Carry this message... Carry...
?!
Golly, what a magnificent bone!... It's certainly a five-star model!... What a bone!
Stay, Snowy! ... Your duty! ... The message!
Stuff and nonsense! The message will keep! But you don't see a bone like that every day!
S.O.S.! HELP!

The message!?!
Vanished!
What will Tintin say?!?
There's only one thing I can do...
To the monastery, double quick! Message or no message, I'll make them follow me.
Half an hour later ...
Here comes the young Lobsang, back from his walk.
Where has that dog come from?... I've never seen him round here before.
Wooah! Wooah!
What does he want with me?... Stop it, you horrid animal!
Come with me! We must save Tintin!
By the White Goddess!... A mad dog!... Help!
Come with me, boy!
Help!... Help!... He- elp!
A mad dog! Help! Help!...
Help! ...
Wooah! Wooah!
We must trap the brute in a corner!
He's cornered!... Careful, now; don't miss him!
Wooah! Grr! Grr! Wooah!

Stop! Do not touch that dog!
?
?
It is undoubtedly Powder Snow, the dog that Blessed Lightning saw in a vision, only a little while ago.
There must be men in danger on the slopes of the White Goddess! We must go and look for them!
You see, we have only to follow him; he shows us the way.
Two days later ...
DONG
DONG DONG DONG
All right! All right! I'm coming!
Come on! Show a leg there! Time we were on our way!
!?
Blistering barnacles, you're a handsome pair!
Obviously we must be in a monastery ...
But how the devil did we end up here?
!?

It's a kite!
Boy monks, flying kites... Not a very serious occupation, I must say!
They're quite happy... while no one seems to be bothering about me! I'd better spy out the land... First of all, where are my boots?
Hey, what the...?! Either my feet have swollen, or my boots have shrunk... They simply won't...
CRACK
!
Thunder-ing typhoons! That's a good start!
Meanwhile...
Welcome, O Travellers, to the monastery of Khor-Biyong... But I thought there were three of you?
They say our friend is still asleep, Grand Abbot... He was completely ex-hausted.
Yes, it seems that you men from other lands have a strange, uncontrollable desire to climb the highest mountains at all costs, even at the risk of your lives. Why is this?
In our case, Grand Abbot, it is not a search for glory, nor a love of climbing that brings us here. Our aim was...
RAT TAT TAT
?
Er... I beg your pardon, but... has anyone got a shoe-horn?

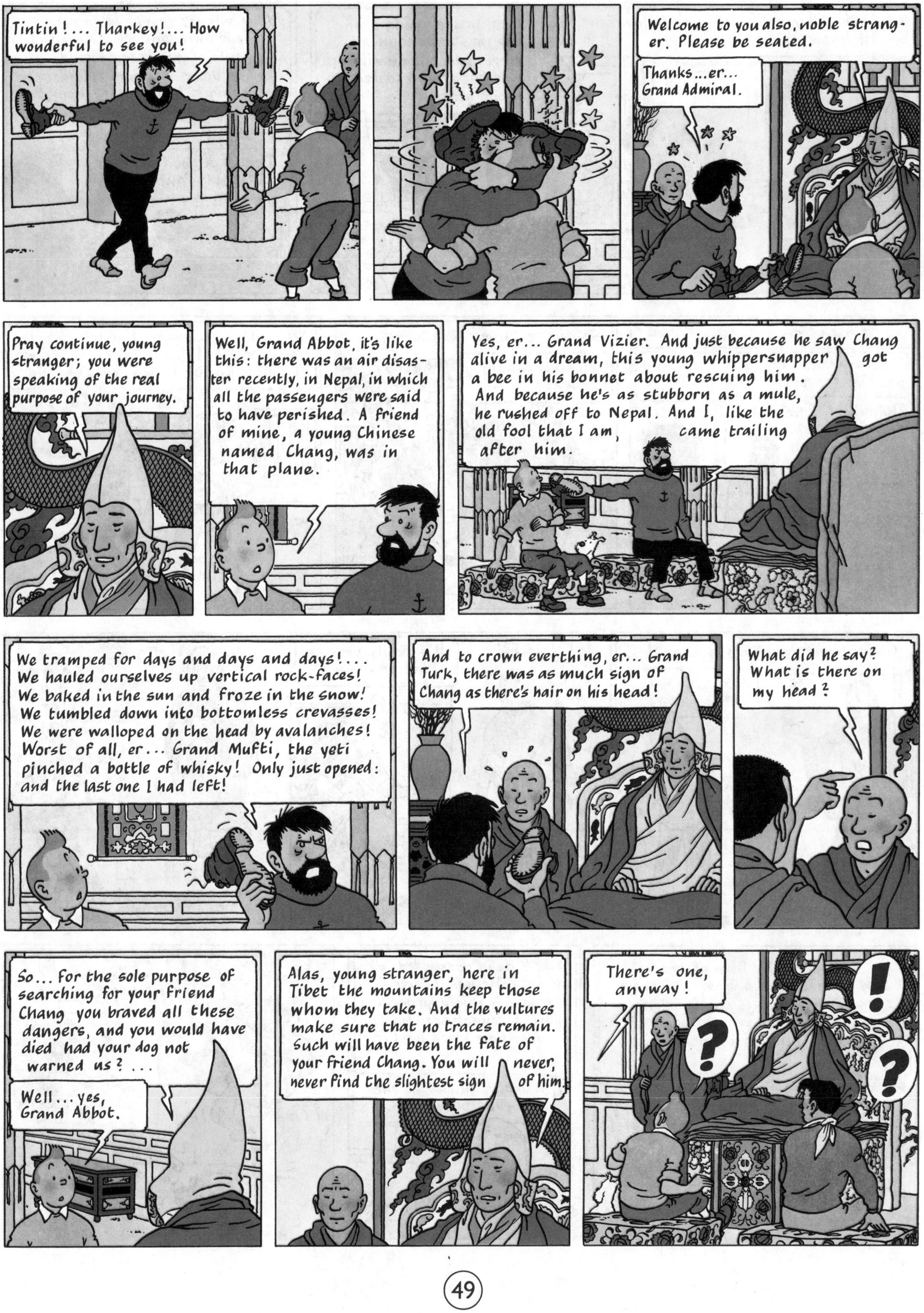
Tintin!... Tharkey!... How wonderful to see you!
Welcome to you also, noble stranger. Please be seated.
Thanks...er... Grand Admiral.
Pray continue, young stranger; you were speaking of the real purpose of your journey.
Well, Grand Abbot, it's like this: there was an air disaster recently, in Nepal, in which all the passengers were said to have perished. A friend of mine, a young Chinese named Chang, was in that plane.
Yes, er... Grand Vizier. And just because he saw Chang alive in a dream, this young whippersnapper got a bee in his bonnet about rescuing him. And because he's as stubborn as a mule, he rushed off to Nepal. And I, like the old fool that I am, came trailing after him.
We tramped for days and days and days!... We hauled ourselves up vertical rock-faces! We baked in the sun and froze in the snow! We tumbled down into bottomless crevasses! We were walloped on the head by avalanches! Worst of all, er... Grand Mufti, the yeti pinched a bottle of whisky! Only just opened: and the last one I had left!
And to crown everthing, er... Grand Turk, there was as much sign of Chang as there's hair on his head!
What did he say? What is there on my head?
So... For the sole purpose of searching for your friend Chang you braved all these dangers, and you would have died had your dog not warned us? ...
Well... yes, Grand Abbot.
Alas, young stranger, here in Tibet the mountains keep those whom they take. And the vultures make sure that no traces remain. Such will have been the fate of your friend Chang. You will never, never find the slightest sign of him.
There's one, anyway!
?
!
?

And the other one's going to follow suit, or I'll know the reason why!
Yes, brave young man, you must abandon all hope; never again will you see the friend so dear to your heart...
Your wisest course is to return to your own country... Moreover, the rule of our order forbids us to harbour strangers. Tomorrow a caravan leaves here, bound for Nepal. May I invite you to join it?
That's a good idea, er ... Grand Panjandrum.
The next morning...
The caravan is ready to leave, noble travellers.
Thank you, Reverend Father. We're quite ready. We'll follow you.
So, we're on our way home...
Without Chang, alas!
Yes, without Chang... but what could you expect? It was hopeless from the start, Tintin. I always said so.
Great Heart, you have forgotten this!
Why, it's Chang's scarf.
It's really very kind of you...
!?!
I see... I see... the horn of the yak. Below, the eye ... a cave ... I see ... I see a boy... this scarf belongs to him... He is lying on a couch of juniper branches...
Impossible! There must be a catch in it!
Alas! He is possessed by devils... He has a fever... But who is this approaching him? I cannot see clearly ... Ah, now I see better ...it...
A photo, quick; no one will ever believe us.
OOOOH! THE MIGOU!

Pity! Too late to snap the flying father! He's come down to earth!
Quick, tell me, where is Chang?
Where is who?
Chang! Chang!... The boy you saw lying on the juniper branches... Where is he?
I do not understand what you mean... Please, you left this scarf... Go in peace, young traveller.
But...
He saw Chang! Obviously ill, but alive! I'm sure of it!
?
Tintin, for heaven's sake! Surely to goodness you don't believe in that flying saucer? He was talking a lot of mumbo-jumbo!
I'm certain it was real!
Come on! We must see the Grand Abbot.
Must have a screw loose!
The Horn of the Yak... There is a mountain of that name, three days' march from here, near the village of Charahbang. What more did he say?
He mentioned an eye, and a cave.
Billions of blistering barnacles, don't tell me you're taking all this hocus-pocus seriously!
You must know, noble stranger, that many things occur here in Tibet which seem unbelievable to you men of the West.
Then he described my friend Chang, lying on a bed of branches. He saw someone approaching Chang, and then, as though terrified, he shouted: "The migou!"... What did he mean by the migou?...
The migou?... You are sure you heard aright: the migou? It is the name given here to the Abominable Snowman. In Nepal they call it the yeh-teh, or yeti; here it is the mi-gou.
But then... Grand Abbot?
Do not enter. He is speaking with the strangers.
Then it would be better if your friend were dead, for he is a prisoner of the migou. And the migou never surrenders his prey!
!
?

Chang a prisoner of the Abominable Snowman!! ... But that's dreadful!... We simply must save him, Grand Abbot!
Alas, it is impossible, Great Heart. No one would run such a risk.
Very well, I'll go alone if necessary. My friend is in danger. You can't expect me to desert him now.
No! You shan't go! Neither alone, thundering typhoons, nor with me! You got round me once, but it won't happen again!... There's been enough skylarking! I won't have any more! You'll come home to Marlinspike with me, blistering barnacles, and there's an end to it!
Just where is this mountain they call the Horn of the Yak?
Say something to him, Grand... Grand... Grand Father!... Make him give up this crazy idea!
Near the village of Charahbang, three days' march from here... There, only a few days ago, a yak was killed by the migou.
There, you see!
Listen, Captain, don't be angry with me... I'm leaving tomorrow for Charahbang. You go with Tharkey and rejoin the caravan... You must understand: I can't do otherwise.
All right, you do as you please! Go as far as you like and look for this Chang of yours! You can go to Mars for all I care! I'm packing my bags and going home...
... before someone gets hurt!
Charahbang - three days later.
A stranger! A stranger!
Hello!... Hello!... Could you take me to the village headman?
You come! You come!
Guide?... To go to Horn of Yak?... No one, Koucho, no one!... Horn of the Yak... Migou!... Migou!
There!
Look!
Another one!
?

You little scallywags! ... Is that what they teach you in school, eh?...
Impossible! I must be dreaming!
Same to you, cheeky!
!
Captain! ... You, here!!!
Yes... and would you believe it: this bunch of young scamps - they had the nerve to put out their tongues at me!
But of course, Captain: that's how you greet people in Tibet... Now, tell me what you're doing here... I thought...
Oh... you... you're surprised, eh?... Well, you see...
Er... I... you... I'd kept the camera... so I thought... I said to myself: I'll take it to him. The Grand Piano lent me horses, and a guide...
How kind of him... And you're going straight back?
Er... you know, since I'm here I think I may as well go a little of the way with you...
Oh, that'd be wonderful... But I haven't found anyone yet to take me... to take us to the Horn of the Yak.
Horn of the Yak?! ... Not go there, Koucho! ... Not go! ... Migou up there; migou! ... Last week him kill yak, just near village!
Where abouts? Could you show me?
An hour later...
Here, Koucho... Here shepherd found yak dead, killed by migou.
This is it! Look, Captain! We don't need a guide: Snowy will show us the way. He's picked up the scent already.
You've been very kind, bringing us this far... Run back home now... Goodbye, my friend. And thank you.
You not go! ... Migou kill you!
Goodbye... Tibetan style! ... NNH!
Off we go, on the last lap! ...
Yah!

GNAAAAH!
Hey Captain, what's up? Are you coming?
Yes, I'm coming...
... but that young monkey needed a lesson in good manners!
The next morning...
What a hope! You're just going to stumble on the den of this teddy-bear, I suppose? It'd be a miracle!
It would if we had nothing to go on... But thanks to Snowy, we're on the right track... Now then, our next objective is a mountain that looks like a yak's horn.
Easy to talk!
There!... What did I tell you?... See... it's unmistakable: that mountain there. Look at the shape!
We must try to arrive at the foot of the mountain at nightfall, and make sure our tent is well hidden.
Three days later...
Look here, Tintin, I'm getting fed up! Here we've been for three days, waiting for this confounded migou of yours to poke his nose out... Besides...
The monk, Blessed Lightning, said the eye. You remember, Captain: the eye below the horn. We must keep watching the eye... Patience, Captain, patience!
Patience!... For all we know, we might sit here waiting for seven years!... If I could even have a good smoke... But no. Poor delicate little fellow... his nose is so sensitive! I don't mind telling you...
HAWAAAW!

The yeti! I can see it! It's just come out from behind a rock, over there!
It's going... It's disappeared. This is it - now's our chance. Come on, Captain! Not a moment to lose!
What can we do?
Go straight to his den - to rescue Chang! Come on!... Hurry!
You... I... don't forget the camera...
Think!... If you could get a photograph of the yeti, imagine what a sensation it would cause!
I'll try.
Stop!
You stay here and keep a look-out. If you see him coming back, give a whistle!
O.K.... Remember the photograph!
!
The entrance to the cave!
I should never have let him go alone... I only hope nothing goes wrong...

Chang!... Chang!...
!
Who...who's there?... Who is it?
Chang!... Chang!... It's me!... It's Tintin!
Chang!... My poor Chang!...
Tintin!
I knew I'd find you in the end!... This is wonderful!
Tintin! Oh, how often I've thought of you!
But you're ill; you're shaking with fever... Come, we must hurry. Wrap yourself up in my anorak and we'll go.
No, Tintin, I can't!
I haven't the strength to move... Besides, supposing he comes back.
There's no danger. One of my friends is waiting outside. Any sign of the yeti, and he'll whistle...
?
He... Why didn't I hear him coming?... Qu-qu-quick... I must whistle...
FFFH
PPPH
ZZZ
WWH
Lean on me - hold tight. You'll see, we'll manage.
TINT...BGLLB...TINTIN! LOOK OU-U-U-U-T!
?!

GRHAWAARH
Help! Fire! Murder! Whatever shall I do?
HAWAARRH!
Action stations! Full steam ahead! Charge!
HWAAARRH!
!?
Hang on, Tintin!... Here I come!...

Captain!... Captain!... Heavens! Are you hurt?
An atom bomb! An atom bomb!
What happened?... An atom bomb, wasn't it?... Are we all dead?
No, it was the yeti. Here, get up.
Quick! Chang's there! We must carry him to the camp at once. The yeti was blinded by the flash-bulb, but he may come back.
Two hours later...
Well, I'd better tell you the whole of my story...
VT-DRO
AIR INDIA
I caught the plane from Patna to Katmandu. It was glorious weather, and everyone on board was very cheerful. But, shortly before we were due to arrive, we ran into a violent storm.
The aircraft was tossed all over the place, and although the crew did their best to reassure us, we feared the worst. Then suddenly there was a terrible crash... and I blacked out...
When I came to I was lying in the snow. My legs hurt dreadfully. Wreckage of every description was littered all around me...
Except for the wind, there wasn't a sound; not a shout, nothing... I was the sole survivor of that horrible disaster!
Panic-stricken, I struggled to my feet. I didn't feel the pain; I had only one thought: to get away. At last, at the end of my strength, I found a niche in the rock. There, I fainted again...
How long I remained unconscious I don't know. But when I came round, I almost died of fright...
In the half-light of a cave, an enormous head was looming over me, and two gleaming eyes were staring at me...
HAW-HAWAOUOUH!

HAWAAO UOUH!
What a heart-rending cry! You'd think he was in distress.
It's not very surprising... He seemed to become quite fond of me. At first he brought me biscuits he found in the wreckage of the plane. Later I lived on plants and roots he brought back from his nightly prowls.
Sometimes he brought me little animals. It was revolting, but I forced myself to eat them... Little by little I regained my strength, until I could stand. Then I had the idea of carving my name on a rock.
Yes, we found the cave, Chang, and saw the stone with your name on it. Then, later, we found your scarf.
Oh, yes, my scarf. I'll tell you about that...
One morning, the yeti came rushing back. He seemed very frightened. He picked me up, and ran off with me in his arms...
Then began that dizzy climb up a sheer cliff!
I was terrified... But he was amazingly sure-footed. Holding on with only one hand, he leaped from rock to rock like a chamois... He stopped for a moment, then I saw what was happening.
Far away, a column of men was heading for the wrecked aircraft... And the yeti was carrying me away from them!
I screamed and yelled to attract their attention. But my voice was too weak. Then I undid my scarf and threw it over the edge, hoping someone would see it and follow our tracks.
That's just what we did, Chang... But what then?
The yeti carried me on. Another storm blew up. I was frozen. I don't know how long that fantastic journey lasted - I was only half-conscious... All I know is...
... I ended up in the cave where you found me, shaking with fever and exhaustion... I was utterly dejected: no one would find me.
I would die there, alone, miserably, far from my family and friends.

Blistering barnacles, I've had enough! I can't bear any more... you'll have to wait while I get my handkerchief.
POOOT
HAWAAAAAAAH!
?
!
?
HAWAAAAAAAAAH!
So there you are, you antediluvian bulldozer!... Come closer, if you dare, you jobbernowl, and I'll turn you into a hearth-rug!
Poor Snowman, what a fright he got. The Captain scared him away when he blew his nose!
MEGACYCLE! PYROMANIAC!
You said "Poor Snowman"... How strange. The only one who knows him, and you don't call him "abominable".
Of course I don't, Tintin: he took care of me. Without him I'd have died of cold and hunger.
A few days later...
The strangers!
The strangers come back!
Yes, here we are, back again... and the migou hasn't eaten us! ... We need porters, to carry this boy to the monastery.
Three days later...
We're nearly there, Chang. You'll soon be on the mend.
Pack up your troubles in your old kitbag and pom pom pom
POM
TOOOT
?
DONG
ZZING
BOOM
TINGALING

The Grand Abbot! It must be something very special, to bring him out in full procession! ...
Greetings, O Great Heart... Following our custom, I present you with this scarf of silk. Blessed Lightning told us of your approach, and I have come to meet you, so that I may bow in deference before you.
Before me, Grand Abbot?... But...
Yes, what you have achieved, few would have dared to undertake. Blessings upon you, Great Heart, for the strength of your friendship, for your courage, and for your steadfastness.
You too, Rumbling Thunder - blessings upon you, for in spite of all, you have the faith that moves mountains.
Moves them? I'd sooner flatten them!
And here is the boy whom you snatched from the jaws of the migou. Blessings upon you, young man, for you inspired great devotion in the hearts of these two strangers.
What about me? Don't I get a word?
Is that thing a trumpet? I suppose you blow in here...
POOAAA!
Oh, sorry!

A week has passed...
How are you feeling now, Chang?
Much better!... A good rest, and being so well looked after - I've completely recovered.
Fine! And thanks to those kind monks who organised this caravan for us, we'll soon be back in Nepal - and then on our way to Europe.
HAWAAAOUH!
!
!
That old reprobate again!
A goodbye from the yeti, Chang... Now he's alone again... until someone from an expedition manages to catch him.
A present from Tibet!
You know, I hope they never succeed in finding him. They'd treat him like some wild animal. I tell you, Tintin, from the way he took care of me, I couldn't help wondering if, deep down, he hadn't a human soul.
Who knows?
The END